T0130523

IT'S ONLY A SMALL WAR

by

Louis Cisneros

Good Morning Vietnam! 1984

Printed in the United States of America.

ISBN: 978-1-4269-4830-5 (sc)
ISBN: 978-1-4269-4831-2 (e)

Trafford rev. 01/31/2011

 www.trafford.com

North America & international
toll-free: 1 888 232 4444 (USA & Canada)
phone: 250 383 6864 ♦ fax: 812 355 4082

To my son Stephen Louis, whom I love

Dad

To all Vietnam Veterans.

A very special dedication to those who lived, to those who died; to those who came back, to those who stayed; to those who gave, to those who suffered.

ACKNOWLEDGEMENT

"Go tell the Spartans, stranger, that here, obedient to their laws, we lie."

Battle of Thermopylae
480 BC
Simonides

CHAPTER 1

Sergeant Robinson looked directly at me and grinned. "Listen up, you sorry scum bag! If you decide to go A.W.O.L., just forget it. Because, I'm going to find you and bring your ass back. If I don't, my ass will be on the line, and I know deep in your heart you don't want that to happen to me, because the whole company will be held responsible for you. That means you'll get some shit from me, and you'll get shit from your buddies."

Two weeks earlier, when I received the letter that changed my life, I didn't know just how bad things could be. Now I know.

"Greetings," the letter read from the Federal Government. "Report to the local Draft Board within the next two weeks or face five years in the Federal Penitentiary."

The summer of 1966 ended tragically for me. I reported to the Oakland Army Terminal for my medical examination. The government gave me a box lunch, and

I was headed south. My final destination was Fort Polk, Louisiana, First Training Brigade, Third Battalion, and Company Delta.

I received my first inside knowledge of some men's sadistic and masochistic natures, the mental and physical strain a human body can endure and the ultimate misuse of the English language.

Fort Polk, the largest Army installation in Louisiana, was overcrowded with raw recruits. The Processing Center there herded the recruits like cattle to the meat market. They administered inoculations for every known disease in the world. My poor arms and cheeks ached even after a few days. We were shipped out in trucks after three days at the Processing Center.

The company was at attention when a burly Sergeant rose to the podium. "My name is Sergeant Robinson. I will be your mother, your father and whoever you want me to be for the next eight weeks. I'm a very religious man, but I cuss a hell of a lot. For the next eight weeks, the United States Government will train and spend its money to make you maggots into soldiers. It's my duty to see that you become good fucking soldiers, because Charlie gonna kick your fucking ass. Get to your buddy next to you, no matter if he's black, white or whatever color, because he might save your asshole. This man's army doesn't want any wet-nosed kids or any fagggots. Is that understood? I didn't hear you fagggoott!"

"Yes Sergeant!"

"You maggots will be assigned platoons and squad leaders. You'll be assigned in alphabetical order, so when I call your name move your ass to your respective platoon. Did you worms understand that?"

"Yes Sergeant!"

"I didn't hear you whores sound off like you have a pair of balls, or did you ladies leave them home with your mama's?"

"No Sergeant!"

"You fucking whores piss me off! Drop and give me ten."

We dropped onto the hot dirty rocks and gave that son of a bitch ten pushups. I felt someone's foot on my back. As I stopped and got up, I got a size twelve in my buttock.

"I said pushups, not assups, Private. Eyes front, Private. You fucking California faggot, I got your number. Drop and give me ten more, scumbag! You look like some big overgrown pussy. My mama can do better than that." That bastard stood over me and grinned.

"I like doing this scumbag. I get my kicks from this."

From the ground up, this man stood nine feet tall. His name tag read Sergeant Morilla. He looked more like a gorilla. Morilla the Gorilla. He looked like Robinson. He was so dark, he was more purple than black. He kicked me and then he hit some other guy who was next to me who was huffing and puffing. He looked like a fat pig Because he was so overweight.

3

Sergeant Morilla had another guy lay on top of this poor slob as he tried doing pushups. He howled at Private Hogan, "See you fat cow, that's the way your girlfriend is getting it. Jody is doing it to her right now. She's creaming like she never did before. You fucking faggot, she got her white legs up in the blue sky touching the clouds."

"Okay scumbag this is just the introduction into the army. There's a lot more where this came from. You bunch of fucking faggots. Listen up! I want you babies to write to your mama and papa. Tell them there will be no more tit sucking. I want everyone to have a letter to your family tomorrow. Do you read me?"

"Yes Sergeant!"

"Okay Scum of the Earth. Get ready for chow. Company. Attention! When I dismiss this company, I want to see assholes running to the chow hall. The last fucking maggot to the chow line better give his soul to the devil, because I am going to destroy your ass. Fall Out!"

There was just dust in Sergeant Robinson's face as we ran toward the chow hall. "And where do you think you're going, Private? I want to have a little talk with you. I want to bite a bone with you."

I was terrified, I could see his red eyes steaming. "Stand at attention when I'm talking to you, Private. Lock those heels."

This is crazy man was all over me, his face thrust into my face. His spit sprayed from his foul mouth all over my face. His Adam's apple bounced up and down, reminding me of a frog that just sat on a water lily croaking. His breath smelled like horse shit.

He had me there for a lifetime with my heels locked, giving me a bunch of shit about the army and what it stood for. "Private Sullivan, the army needs good men like you. Intelligent, bright and with leadership abilities. It could be a good career for a young man like you. That's why I want you to be my Acting Squad Leader. One good thing about being a squad leader in my platoon, there will be no shit details. You'll have weekend passes to Leeville where you can get a cheap fuck. Get your pecker wet for a few dollars. Now isn't that a good deal? Keep that in mind, Private."

"Yes, Sir, I would like that very much," I said enthusiastically.

"Get your ass to the front of the chow line and report to me after you finish."

Sergeant Robinson gave us all the scuttlebutt how he wanted us to handle his platoon, how to give orders for shit details and how to deal with the fuckups. He gave us a demonstration. He made us get down on all fours and kicked our behinds. He said it would make our assholes bigger and our minds smaller. His right boot was called "Sweet Georgia Brown." The left was called "Bitching Mama." Both girls came down hard on my "Rest and Recreation Area."

The next day the sun shone from a cloudless Louisiana sky. The pine trees waved in a gentle breeze that blew from the Gulf of Mexico. The air was filled with a brisk mixture of salt and pine.

Sergeant Robinson got the platoon up at four o'clock that morning. He said we we're worms, so he had us wiggle on the floor of the barracks in our boxer shorts. He screamed at us with us ferocious tone born in his balls, "Get down, you fucking worms. Wiggle like the maggots you are."

Sergeant Robinson stepped over our bodies, sometimes kicking one of us in the ribs. Some of the other men were moaning. He used Sweet Georgia Brown unsparingly on the right side of my neck. "You maggot, didn't I tell you to keep these fucking worms in line? Crawl, you scum of the earth."

After a few hours of crawling under the bunks and latrine, we fell out to the supply room and were issued M-16's. Sergeant Robinson stood staring at us. One wrong move and the ladies would come thundering down. He had his Smokie on. I had to admit he looked good and wore it proudly. On his fatigue shirt he had Airborne Wings and Combat Infantry Badge. Sergeant Robinson had been in the Korean War. Later I learned he was highly decorated.

The following day our ribs were black and blue. He had us come out in full field packs to crawl under the barracks screaming "Kill, kill." He again beat the platoon with his large fists and the two ladies.

I had to administer first aid to Private Garcia. Garcia, a native of Puerto Rico, was just as dark and ugly as

Sergeant Morilla. He said he was Spanish, but he looked black. He didn't have much going for him. He was short, black and ugly. He had abrasions all over his small body. His upper lip was swollen and torn on one side. His ribs were cracked from one of the ladies.

By late evening, half the platoon was exhausted from the running and the petty shit that he did to us. My muscles were aching from head to toe. That jerk made us duckwalk wearing a full field pack. He made us chant a demanding phrase over and over again.

"Quack, quack, quack, quack
I'm a silly little duck
I wiggle my silly little ass.
Quack, quack, quack, quack
I'm a silly little duck
And I don't give a fuck
Quack, quack, quack, quack"

Private Garcia said, "Duck in Puerto Rico means queer, and I'm not doing it any more."

Sergeant Robinson came down on Garcia like a ton of shit. Smack! Garcia flew like a butterball down the middle of his bunk. Garcia had a monstrous cut on the side of his head. Most of his right ear was drooping. Sergeant Robinson stood over him using Sweet Georgia Brown on his ribs and butt. "You black nigger." Garcia stumbled and fell on the floor once more from a kick to the solar plexus that made him vomit. The mixture of clotted blood and chipped beef on toast was nauseating.

"You see Private Garcia left you a birthday present. Get up, you protozoa!"

There were tears in Garcia's eyes. He stood on his knees, holding his stomach.

I rushed over to him and helped him to his bunk. "Come on, Garcia, don't don't let that prick get you in trouble. Can't you see that's what he wants?"

"Private Sullivan! Remember, this pussy fell in the shower. Any complaints to the Old Man will be on my shit list for the duration of training. Did you get that Private?"

Sergeant Robinson and Sergeant Morilla walked around during the beginning of our bayonet training. |They brandished sticks which they used on our heads and rib cages.

"Kill, kill, you maggots!" Smash! "This is the way you do it! You beat your enemy without mercy!" Boom!

Sergeant Robinson struck a recruit on the side of the ear. While he was on the ground, he slammed the stick in his midsection. "Goddamn that's the way you kill your enemy. Knock his fucking head off!"

Man, he's insane, I thought.

"What's the bayonet for, you bunch of maggots?" Sergeant Robinson raised his stick high over his head.

"Kill, kill!"

Dear Dad,

I'm sorry it's taken me so long to write you back, but you know how it is in basic training. I am so tired of marching and running, I don't even have time to dream. Tell Mom that the skivvies were nice, but the stripes were kinky. I'll promise to write more as soon as I can. There are about two more weeks for training, and I should go to Airborne training at Fort Benning, Georgia.

Dad, I got into some trouble a few days ago. A few of the guys went A.W.O.L – Private Garcia and some other Puerto Ricans from the First Platoon. They ripped off some of the other guys' valuables. I didn't turn him in for two days. The company was given a twenty-four hours pass. They didn't come back.

They were caught in Georgia. They're in the stockade. I might never see those guys again. I guess I never felt so bad about what I had done. Well, Dad, this is all for now.

Your son,
Charlie

A week later, Private Garcia came into the barracks. "Garcia, how is it going?" How was the stockade?" I asked anxiously.

"That fucking Sergeant Robinson just kicked me in the ass with the two ladies. Man that was nothing. My father in Puerto Rico kicks harder. I just got an Article Fifteen and was fined fifty dollars from my pay."

"That's all?"

"Well, what the hell did you want them to do to me? Put me in a dungeon, strip me down and give me twenty lashes on my balls?"

"Hey man. I'm just concerned for you. Look, aren't we friends? Get that chip off your shoulder, Okay? Hey man your stuff is in my room. Let's go get it. Okay?"

The last two weeks were unbearable. We were constantly running and marching. We had to face the toughest challenge of all – the Infiltration Course. We crawled under barbed wire while some nut shot above our heads with a fifty as we were belly–down in the mud. We were becoming soldiers. The last seven weeks were hell.

At last, graduation on Friday and we cleaned the barracks for the final inspection. Twenty–four hours later, most of the guys would be going home for two weeks. Almost everyone knew where they would be reporting to their next station.

Fort Benning was my next destination, where I would have four weeks of training to become a paratrooper. I was beginning to enjoy the army. I felt proud wearing the uniforms and what it stood for. I was a little skeptical of killing a human being, but if the opportunity came I would be ready mentally and physically. God is on my side. I knew I might end up in Southeast Asia, and perhaps I might even get killed.

Sergeant Robinson walked up the second floor of the barracks and stood in the center of the floor. The red floor shined and sparkled, because we had just waxed it. His double reflected on the mirror-like floor. His twin stood as tall as he did, and looked just as mean and evil.

"Front and center, you shitbirds. You, too Rican," he called to Private Garcia. "Move your ass nigger. You're a nigger aren't you?"

Private Garcia ran to Sergeant Robinson. He stood straight in his skivvies. He was just a breath from his face. For a few seconds, I was afraid Garcia would punch Sergeant Robinson. Instead he stood up straight, face to face with his enemy. "Yes, Sergeant Robinson, I'm a nigger just like you. The only difference is that I'm a Puerto Rican nigger."

"No shit, You fucking Rican." Sergeant Robinson moved by him and smiled. Sweet Georgia Brown and Bitching Mama walked right by the rest of the men. He walked toward the stairway and shouted, "Viva Puerto Rico!"

I felt like a ton of shit fell off me when I heard that. A feeling of pride went through my body. I am an American, the best, the greatest.

Later that evening, Sergeant Robinson called the entire platoon together. "I want to congratulate you soldiers. I'm proud of you and privileged to have trained a bunch of good men. You're the best I've trained."

"What a bunch of shit he's giving us," I whispered to the man next to me. "He says that to all the recruits who go through here."

"I want you soldiers to look good tomorrow morning when we pass in review. Remember, the Post Commander,

Major General James H. Skeldon, will be there. There will be some dignitaries from the Department of the Army. So look good."

Saturday morning, the sun was shining, and the warm breeze blew up from the gulf. The humidity was tolerable. Occasionally cerulean clouds pierced through the darker rain clouds. The blue reminded me of Barbara Miller, my old girlfriend. She had big blue eyes and miniature freckles on her pug nose. Her lips were a beautiful shade of red. I remember that night before I was inducted in the army. It seemed a lifetime ago.

I closed my eyes, and deep in my mind, there she was. That night I picked her up and she stood in the doorway of her parents' house, smiling beautifully. She came out from the house with a red tight sweater, tight slacks and a red scarf around her neck. We walked toward the car hand in hand. Tears rolled down her beautiful cheeks. She kissed my lips. She grabbed me around the neck and laid her head on my shoulder. "I'll wait for you," she whispered.

We drove to our favorite place, the Almaden Dam. I drove in a Kwik Stop to get a six-pack of Budweiser. As we drove away, I pulled off an easy pulltop and threw it out the window.

After a few hours at the dam and five beers, I had more than the army in mind. Every time I looked at her, my groin throbbed. I started the car and coasted down the winding road. I was feeling high and a little horny. "Let's get some more beer and get a hotel room so we can talk in private." Actually I just wanted to get her drawers down. "Okay?" I asked devilishly.

She didn't answer, just stood starting toward the night-lights. I would have given my whole ninety dollars the army gave me to know what she was thinking.

"What do you say, honey?" I repeated. "Let's get a hotel room."

An hour later, I got a room at the El Rancho Inn on South Thirteen. The night manager was a skinny Mexican. I paid twenty-five dollars for a large single room. We walked down a long set of stairs to doorway number five. He gave me the key and smiled. "Go to it boy. It's time to become a man."

We entered the room, and the dark carpet and black walls absorbed us. At the rear of the room was a large mirror on the ceiling and along the two walls adjoining the bed. Huge pillows lay on the bed on the floor. My best fantasies were about to come true. I had a roaring erection, and my fly was about ready to explode. I watched her undress. My eyes did a quick survey and enjoyed what I was going to have. I stared at her body,, as she moved toward the bed. The movement of her nude body reflected in the mirrors caught my eyes, sending a shudder of excitement through my insides. As she walked toward me, her breasts bounced from left to right with each step. They were round and ripe. Her nipples were as large as silver dollars. I slipped between the satin sheets as she moved her warm body next to mine.

By three a.m., we were exhausted from lovemaking.. I was grateful for the bit of freedom we shared. That moment I will cherish for the rest of my life.

"Hey Sullivan. Sergeant Robinson wants to give you the scuttlebutt. Hey asshole. Wake up."

There was no point dreaming about the past. Man what nipples she had. Well let me think about them a few more seconds....

Early that day, the company fell out for the last reveille dressed in our khakis. Our boots were split-shined. Khakis were pressed straight. We were showered and smooth-shaven, ready to march to the parade ground. The whole brigade marched over for our final pass. The moment came two hours later.

"Company. Attention. Right face."

CHAPTER 2

The Vietnamese have their own Zodiac. Legend states that on a certain New Year's Day ages ago, Buddha called all animals of the world to him. He promised that those who paid homage would receive a Gift. As a mark of honor, they would be given a year which would be thereafter named for them.

People who were born under the sign of the horse were popular, cheerful and skillful with money. They are wise and talented and are good with their hands. Horse people aren't noted for their patience. They are hot-blooded, but in their everyday work they can be dispassionate over what they do. During the first and second phases of their life, horse people will have a good life.

Two months later I was sent to Vietnam with all expenses paid by the U.S. Government. I was born during the year of the horse eighteen years before in nineteen forty-six. My first phase in life was to begin somewhere in Southeast Asia.

I looked down at Vietnam from a bird's eye view for the first time. It looked peaceful and beautiful. There was no sign of war as I looked down on the mountainous shore and the valleys of rice fields beside the turquoise sea. We landed in Cam Ranh Bay and I wondered about ground fire as the C-130 made its final descent. We were greeted by Screaming Eagles from the 101st Airborne. They had driven ten miles with open arms. We were their long-awaited replacements, and they greeted us royally.

As darkness fell, the guns' distant thunder reminded me that I was in a combat zone. Bright flares illuminated the sky every few minutes. All the Eagles seemed serious and committed to the war. They were frightened. We were there so stop communism.

Cam Ranh Bay was a small port city of many contrasts. There were small beach huts, French restaurants and a Post Exchange. There were hordes of people, especially young boys selling Coca-Cola packed in ice and rice to keep it cold. We were told to travel in small parties as protection against the Viet Cong tossing live grenades.

During the next two days, we were trucked deep into the bush, accompanied by heavy armored trucks, 106 millimeter recoilless rifles, fifties mounted on Jeeps. It was serious business. We arrived five hours later at the fortified command post of the 101st Airborne Division.

I was to be assigned to the First Brigade, Charlie Company, of the Second of the Five O Deuce. I later learned that the division was only a few kilometers from the Laotian border. I had the uneasy feeling that I would be out there shortly with no hope to come back to the real world. . .

Paratroopers sat around in and out of bunkers close to home in case of incoming rounds. The place looked dingy, like Fox-Hole City. It was a city of bunkers, holes and sandbags. Most of the men looked tired and bewildered.

Some unshaven Eagle, no more than eighteen years old, came up to the deuce and a half and said, "Are you the replacements? We sure need some bodies. Charlie zapped a few last night in a firefight."

"Here are my orders," I said as I began to shake. I felt like I was going to vomit. "The old man isn't here. He's at the command post with the Battalion Commander," the pimply trooper said.

Later, I met my new Platoon Sergeant, Sergeant Baker; he was a tall black man in his late twenties who looked more like forty. He smelled like shit. He needed a bath badly. He studied our orders, and his smell hit me like a bullet between the eyes. His fatigues were dirty and torn. His week-long beard and sores on his face gave me impression that it was going to be hell. My God, please help me get out of here in one piece.

I learned later that Baker's Platoon had just returned from a reconnaissance patrol the night before. They lost three men on that patrol. The long hump in the dense jungle took its toll on Sergeant Baker and the platoon.

The paratroopers sprawled around the outpost as we walked toward the command post, which was a small hut constructed from bamboo and palm fronds. A colony of bunkers surrounded the Captain's hut. There were foxholes everywhere I looked. The men looked like prairie dogs in fatigues. Some of the troopers were cleaning their sixteens. Some were lying around talking. A few were shaving from their steel pots.

The strain of combat and the hot sun showed on Sergeant Baker's face. The strain he was under showed in his every moment. His eyes were bloodshot. The skin on his face and neck were prime rib to the insects, especially the mosquitoes and ants. Sergeant Baker had a pleasant way of making us at home even in such a God-forsaken place. He handed me a box of C-Rats with pork and beans with franks. Later I learned that the rations were his private stock. The box lunch had a miniature toilet paper roll, a pack of four cigarettes, two square-shaped sticks of gum, fruit and two cans of food, which weren't bad considering I ate them cold.

Sergeant Baker had a southern accent, which made it difficult to interpret what he was saying half the time. He sounded like he was from Louisiana or Georgia. I knew instinctively that I would stick to him like glue. It was the first time in my life I was frightened. He gave us the scuttlebutt on the Viet Cong and our position in Southeast Asia.

After we finished our four-course meal, Sergeant Baker gave us a grand tour of the compound. The tour terminated at the supply room, where they issued me a pair of jungle boots, a sixteen and the rest of the equipment.

"Okay, I don't want anyone trying to be a hero and get yourself or someone else killed. Listen to all instructions that are given to you." Sergeant Baker continued giving his expertise on military strategies. "I don't want any John Waynes. This is the real thing, not some movie. Here, Private, see if you can pull this pin with your teeth."

He gave me a fragmentation grenade. I felt stupid with the grenade in my mouth. "We don't want anyone to think that he can win this war by himself. Heroes die young. People are dying in this war. Even the village whores are killing soldiers."

The small group of men started laughing at Sergeant Baker's remark. "Don't think they're fucking you to death. The gook whores are putting broken tips of cola bottles in their cunts. They carry plastic cyanide pills in their mouths for you lover boys." That got a ten-four from the group.

"We've found men out in the rice paddies with their balls in their mouths. You people have to learn all this today, this very second. Tomorrow will be too late. See this sixteen? Carry it always. Take care of it like it's your peter. Because if you lose it, you're fucked. Take it to sleep. Take it when you have to take a shit. Jack off with it. Play with it. Do whatever you want with it, but keep it at your side. It's the only friend you've got out here in the bush. The old man should be here tomorrow to brief the company on the next mission. The scuttlebutt is that it will be the largest search and destroy operation since the war started. Any questions?" Sergeant Baker asked.

I had a large lump in my throat, and I was numb from the waist down. I felt like I was bolted to the ground. Sweat dripped from my forehead. The salty river of perspiration irritated my eyes. My right hand reached out toward my crucifix and grasped it. My God, I beg you help me through this hell I'm in.

"Our Father, who art in heaven, hallowed be thy name. Thy kingdom come, Thy will be done on earth as it is heaven. Give us this day our daily bread and forgive our trespasses as we forgive those who trespass against us. Lead us not into temptation, but deliver us from evil. Amen"

The sixteens were light in weight, black and had a hand grip for easy carrying. It was totally different from the one I used in basic training. This one was going to kill real people. It had more firepower and real bullets. The sixteen's impact was like a ricochet. The sixteen had its drawbacks, too. It was made from plastic and sometimes jammed. They issued six Fully loaded magazines with every round a tracer – two bandoliers, one concussion grenade and one fragmentation grenade. I felt like a walking arsenal.

The following day, early in the evening, five choppers landed fifty yards outside the perimeter. The blades from the hueys blew dirt, weeds and water buffalo shit in our faces. Gases from the red flares drifted into the camp as eight paratroopers emerged. They were obscured by the fog. It reminded me of The Walking Dead with Vincent Price. Their bodies were hidden by the red fog, and then

20

out of the mist four bodies emerged. The soldiers held their hands on their helmets to keep them from blowing off by the blades. Three paratroopers wore tiger fatigues and didn't look like Americans. They were Vietnamese Paratroopers.

The tall good-looking man was Captain America, as the men called him. Later, I learned why. He had come up from the ranks. He was field commissioned in 1963 in Vietnam. He was commissioned from a platoon leader to a Second Lieutenant. Captain America was wounded in action in Vietnam and was decorated with a Silver Star, Bronze Star and Purple Heart. He was hit in a French sugar cane field. Even after he was hit in the right arm, he managed to toss a hand grenade at the Viet Cong.

Captain America was in his early forties with a touch of light gray hair. He stood six foot and a solid two hundred pounds. He got his name from his company several years earlier. He didn't fool around with the local women, nor did he drink or smoke. He still could outrun and out-march any paratrooper, young or old. He was also religious. He carried a small pocket bible in his left pocket, close to his heart. He made all the men pray before a major operation or patrol.

I stood in front of Captain America, eyes front and my heels locked straight, at attention. "At ease soldier," he said. The impeccable man saluted and smiled. "Are you a replacement? If so, please don't salute. You might get me killed. No saluting in the field." I could see that he was serious about staying alive.

"Sergeant Baker, we need bodies out in the field. The new men can start on short patrols tomorrow. Rest the other men tomorrow. I want these men to alleviate the duties from the rest of the men. Have them pull guard tonight for a few hours. I want them to get used to it."

"Yes Sir." Sergeant Baker answered.

"Okay men, Sergeant Baker will assign you to a squad in each platoon in the company. May God be with you."

I was assigned to the first platoon under Sergeant Baker. He had the First Rifle Team. The squad leader was Sergeant Roberto De La Cruz, a Mexican-American from Tucson, Arizona. He, like the rest of the team, had sores all over his face and arms. The rest of the squad members were PFC Cook from Mobile, Alabama, PFC Garcia from Houston, Texas, SP/ 4 Juan Hinojosa from San Juan, Puerto Rico, PFC Davis from Baton Rouge, Louisiana, and PFC Hanson from Kansas.

Home was a few half-shelters with bamboo and palm fronds, a few foxholes around the hut and a large bunker. A few scorpions and large red ants kept us company. The squads in the platoon were undermanned. The platoon still needed a few more good souls. The Cong zapped too many good men in the last two months. Replacements were still needed in all the platoons of the company.

Hours later, during the late evening, Private Cook came up to me. "Your watch is from midnight till O two hundred. Why don't you go down the hill to watch the movie?"

"What's playing?" I asked surprised they had movies in that God- forsaken place.

"Combat, with Vic Morrow and Rich Jason. Bring your web gear and sixteen. I have a few C rations – hamburger in a can. Keep the box for a letter. Stationery is hard to come by." He showed me how it was done as we walked down the hill. He cut the ends off the box and folded in the middle and used flour and water to make a paste.

He stuck both ends together and it became an envelope and a letter in one. We walked down the hill as the moon fell between the clouds.

CHAPTER 3

The morning sun glared with its tropical force. The humidity and heat were almost unbearable. Small insects were out in force. The air was filled with the odor of gunpowder. Gunpowder was beginning to be a common smell, like the gooks working in the rice fields.

De La Cruz was the first in the chow line where they did not have C rations for breakfast. Perspiration from my forehead dripped into my ham and eggs as I stirred it with a stick. The chow hall was a tent with big metal pots hanging outside. I grabbed De La Cruz' bottle of Puerto Rican hot sauce to help kill the taste of the eggs. He made it from Vietnamese herbs.

He said, "Use some, Sullivan. It kills tapeworms and intestinal infections, and it makes your asshole bigger."

After the Puerto Rican torture I endured that morning, I could eat anything the army served.

Sergeant Baker approached and sat on a large pot. "Come here, you two. You're going on a detail, so get some ammo and your sixteen."

We started walking toward the Jeep that had a sixty mounted on it. Across the rice paddy two hundred yards away, there was movement of men with heavy weapons pointing north. The long tube exploded, and a shell hit and exploded in the side of a small hill. They were just target practicing.

"Private, do you know how to feed this weapon?" Sergeant Baker asked.

"No Sergeant. I never fired that weapon before." I jumped behind the Jeep. "I never qualified with the sixty," I said quietly.

"Well, get you ass behind it and hold on. You're about to become familiar with this weapon. See those cans?" He pointed toward some ammo cans on the side of the Jeep. "Those cans hold two hundred rounds each. Grab a single belt and pull the cover up and place it there and pull the lever back and let it go."

I did what he said.

"See, you're an expert."

De La Cruz nodded and lit a cigarette. "You fucking dumb private." De La Cruz allowed himself a small smile. "Didn't they teach you to fire the sixty?"

The artillery fired once more at the small hill, this time sending a large mushroom of white phosphorus.

The countryside was spectacular. Some of the small huts in the village were made from beer cans. Budweiser led in popularity in the construction business. The runner up was Falstaff. It reminded me of Tijuana. C ration boxes were in third with a combination of bamboo and palm fronds. Sergeant Baker stopped at a large hut that was more sturdily constructed than most. I thought a rich person lived there, but much to my surprise, it was the local whorehouse.

Sergeant Baker beeped the horn, and two beautiful young girls came out. They were no more than sixteen, and they wore sexy black pajamas.

Sergeant Baker asked one of the girls. "Where's Mamasan?"

They waved their hands to follow them into the tin establishment and for five dollars we could get the Viet Cong special and a trip to the local witch doctor for penicillin.

Baker and De La Cruz stepped down and went into the building. Their laughter echoed in the tin building. Later, I learned they both were in business with the madam. They used their ration cards to buy what she needed to keep the boys happy. They got a healthy profit from their venture.

Thirty minutes later, De La Cruz and Baker came out with large smiles on their dirty faces. They had their arms around a couple of those lovely creatures. "Hey Private, front and center."

I pulled the plate from the machine gun and jumped down from the Jeep. "Yes Sergeant," I said.

"Which one of these do you want? To my right is Minnie and to my left is Susie."

I stood there with my mouth open.

"Come on boy, get some snatch. Get your peter wet. It's on the house, a free sample. It's good stuff. I know. See. Susie show him your tits."

They were a beautiful mouthful.

"I don't think so Sergeant," I said reluctantly.

"You're learning, boy. You're learning." He laughed. "Well, girls, he doesn't want you. Sin Loy."

After a few minutes on the dusty road, Baker and De La Cruz gazed into infinity, riding high on a cloud of cannabis. We passed beer can city. A gust of wind swooped down on the Jeep as five water buffaloes moved into the middle of the road. Sergeant Baker's eyes were dilated and watery as he stopped the Jeep and jumped in the back. "Move over, Private." Sergeant Baker almost fell over an ammo box. He slammed a two- hundred-round belt in the sixty. "This is the way to kill gooks, Private." Sergeant Baker fired a burst of six pounds with the sixty, tracers hitting a mound in rice paddy. Three rounds hit a small grave in the middle of the rice paddy. "Okay Private, it's your turn." He wanted me to shoot some old Vietnamese man. "Shoot him in the asshole, Private."

"I can't do that Sergeant," I said, frightened.

"Sure you can. Watch me. Move over Private."

He grabbed the machine gun and knocked me over the side of the Jeep. Bang, bang, bang. The bullets hit the grave. The peasant continued plowing. Sergeant De La Cruz pulled out a few joints and placed them on his tongue and started rolling them up and down.

"Hey, Sarge, you're gonna kill that old gook. Here I'll role one for you. It's a bomber." He laughed at me like I was crazy.

Sergeant Baker jumped off the Jeep and started throwing beer cans at the water buffaloes. "C'mon man, let's get out of here before they send us to the nut house."

I was relieved when we passed Tin Can Alley. It was like a Charlie Chaplin comedy. Two Vietnamese Military Police were behind us. Sergeant Baker hit a cartful of coconuts and small melons. The villager ran behind the Jeep, calling us names. The military police were on our tail, squashing melons right behind us. Sergeant Baker and De La Cruz, still drinking beer, pulled out their forty-fives and placed them on their laps.

De La Cruz pulled out a Tiger Thirty-three, a Vietnamese beer from inside his right pocket, and opened it with his teeth. The tiger wasn't the greatest beer in the world, but it caused intoxication. He swallowed it in one gulp, got up on the seat and threw it at the MPs. Sergeant Baker stopped the Jeep and jumped back to the sixty, pulled the lever and let it slam ready to fire.

"Move over, fool, and get your weapon. The enemy is on us!" Sergeant Baker screamed at me.

Baker with a joint in his mouth and the sixty moving back from side to side, asked the two MPs, "What the fuck you chinks want?"

"Didi Mau you fucking gook!"

De La Cruz had his forty-five ready for a shoot-out at the Old Katy's Corral. The young Vietnamese began to sweat and got enough spit to ask Sergeant Baker for one hundred and fifty piasters for the damage. Sergeant Baker answered back, "Dung Dau, you fucking gooks, we're not paying no money. Your Dinky Dau."

De La Cruz moved over to the side of the Jeep. The other Vietnamese had his carbine aimed at Baker. De La Cruz aimed his forty-five at the Vietnamese in the Jeep. Baker and De La Cruz were serious about what they were doing. The Vietnamese broke his nerve and ran behind the Jeep. Sergeant Baker fired a short burst from the sixty, hitting the tires in front of the jeep. They drove back toward the village with their muffler between their drive shaft. De La Cruz and Baker began to laugh and open some beers. They handed me one of those Tiger Thirty-threes, but what I needed was to change my drawers.

That evening, there was a great commotion about some movie that would be at headquarters – The Cincinnati Kid, with Steve McQueen and Edward G. Robinson. All the card players were high on seeing the movie. That evening paratroopers were coming out of their holes. They were like an army of ants. Some even had six-packs of beer in their hands, with C rations to boot. The film had been swapped for fifty cases of beer from the First Cavalry Division. It was a perfect night to see a flick. The moon was full with few clouds in the sky. It reminded me of the Tropicana Drive-In in good old San Jose, California.

Many trucks and Jeeps arrived with troopers from other companies.

As usual, the projectionist had his head up his ass. The film was on backwards. All the boos and the empty beer cans went up in the air. The animals were restless. After a few minutes, the projectionist finally had the film on the reel and ready to roll.

Some drunk cherry jumped up and hollered, "Airborne all the way, Sergeant!"

There was a heavy barrage of beer cans and C rations at the young man. A small container of jelly hit him on the head and knocked him to the ground.

Midway through the movie I got up and walked to the john in the jungle. There was a strange whistle as I walked back toward the movie. The projectionist moved to focus the movie, and then Boom! Incoming mortars. Boom! Boom! Two more. One hit the screen. The other hit the projectionist. I saw smoke and a large hole where he was standing.

Smoke was everywhere. I was stunned from what I saw. The congregation of troops was moving, crawling in all directions from the scene. The ground rumbled and moved under my feet. The sky lit up with hand flares and eighty millimeters. The night turned into the nightmare with firearms and explosions tearing into the night. Boom! One rocket ignited the fuse dump, turning it into a red and yellow mushroom. Deadly debris from all directions hit the Command Post and the Battalion Aid Station. Three more rockets hit around the side of the ammo dump. A huge puff of yellow smoke and fire filled the dark night. A few hit the perimeter, sending sandbags in the air along with a few bodies.

It took the Viet Cong four minutes to destroy and kill several troopers. The Viet Cong were smart. They hit all the important positions, and they were all direct hits. The incoming mortars stopped. I laid motionless as the smoke drifted toward me. Minutes later, the word came down that it was over. A patrol was coming in three hundred yards away with wounded. The patrol had gone out earlier that evening. Four came out of the bush. Four more with stretchers followed the exhausted leaders. A squad of troopers ran out to protect the incoming patrol. They were crisscrossing in intervals of ten seconds. Minutes later, the squad intercepted their wounded comrades.

From the smoking ruins of the ammo dump to the damaged movie screen and the bunkers, there came a chopping sound from the south. The cobras from the fourth Cavalry lit the sky. The steady chopping sound of the cobra's blades meant a renewal of safety and protection to the troopers.

There were only three choppers. The combatants stared at the dark sky, waiting. The mini-armada circled the perimeter and fired a dose of rockets and the gunners fired at will. They showed no discrimination at what they fired. The cobras swooped down on the enemy at treetop level, sending rockets down on them. The rockets made yellow mushrooms in the dense jungle. The patrol continued through the screen of smoke and small arms fire.

The attack was not caused by the hardcore North Vietnamese Troops but by a handful of Viet Cong.

There were at least two regiments in the vicinity along with the support of the Viet Cong. It was rumored there were about seven thousand troops, and they would start a monsoon offensive.

The site of the movie was a smoldering ruin. The men were scattered or dead.

It was my first taste of combat.

CHAPTER 4

The smell of gunpowder still hung in the air as morning broke between the mountains. It was a beautiful countryside, the towering mountains contrasting with the geometric fields. The rice paddies were deserted. We didn't have to be military geniuses to know why. The concertina was heavily damaged around the perimeter. Bodies from last night's fighting still lay broken and bloody. There were numerous blood trails and blood stains by the tree lines – a few AK-47s lost in the fighting as the enemy retreated.

Sergeant Baker climbed out of his hole in the ground. He called me over. "I have a detail for you, Private. Go and get your gas mask. You'll need it."

I strode slowly down the long narrow patch where the rest of the men were waiting. Most of them were lying on the dirt reading Casper, the Friendly Ghost.

The night before, the Viet Cong destroyed a bridge that isolated a small village from the compound. The small hamlet was about five miles away. By mid-afternoon, we swept the high grass and bush in the morning heat. We found a few dead Viet Cong in the high elephant grass. Their blood-soaked bodies were covered with ants and flies.

We finally reached our destination. Exhausted and dejected, we walked carefully through the dense bush. Punji stakes were an ever-present danger. The stakes were pieces of sharpened bamboo smeared with human excrement. The traps, invisible in the bush, could slice right through a boot.

At the small hamlet, we clicked off our safeties so we would be ready for the unexpected. The patrol twisted through the huts in pairs. Sergeant Baker and I stayed at the entrance to guard the patrol's back. I quickly surveyed the bush in the back and moved with Sergeant Baker. An old papasan came with his hands up to welcome us. He kept smiling, and most of his teeth were stained black and red from the beetle nuts. Lieutenant Nguyen ran to the old gent and started speaking Vietnamese. They were Montagnards.

"Sergeant Baker, there's Yards," Private Hanson said.

Apparently he was the Jefe of the village. Lieutenant Nguyen showed great respect for the old gent. He came to Baker and said in fluent English, "Sergeant, there's a couple of bodies a few yards away from the village. They're Americans."

"Saddle up!" Sergeant Baker said. We walked cautiously through the village. Only a soldier could know that feeling that someone was there who wanted to kill us. The patrol headed north toward the bush, which touched the deep jungle toward the Laotian and Cambodian borders. As the bush grew thicker, the trails became narrower and finally disappeared completely in the tall and thick bushes.

Night fell quickly as the patrol found two nude bodies covered with parasites. My God. They're maggots. All those things were all over their bodies, crawling between their eyes. The stench could turn an elephant twice.

I understood why Sergeant Baker made us bring the gas masks. I threw up three times before I got my mask on. The bodies had no dog tags.

"Okay, I want to see assholes and elbows." We had to bag the corpses and find a clearing and wait for the choppers.

An hour later, we made it to clearing. The squad was hungry and drenched in sweat and in Viet Cong land, a free-fire zone. Baker was concerned that the squad were all cherries. No one was experienced in combat and we were deep in Viet Cong territory.

Baker told us, "Move quickly and quietly."
Move quickly we did. I ran short sprints and moved low between the bushes. We stopped to catch our breath. I always tried to stay close to Baker.

We stumbled across two Vietnamese eating under a tree, about fifty yards from the clearing. They were just as surprised as we were. Sergeant Baker moved like he wanted to stay alive for a long a time.

With his sixteen at waist high, he moved like a jaguar. "Dung Lai. Move sonofabitch, and you'll never eat rice again."

The Vietnamese placed their hands on their heads as Sergeant Baker pointed with his sixteen.

"Search their bags," Baker said.

I ransacked their small camp. There were no weapons, just a couple of water buffaloes. The buffaloes had large bags strapped to their bodies. The cows were carrying heavy burdens on their backs.

"Sergeant, I'm going to check the bags on the water buffaloes, okay?"

"Okay, but be careful when you move the bags. They could be booby-trapped," Baker answered.

The large cows were grazing as I took my bayonet to probe the large bags. I heard a thump in one bag. "Sergeant, I hit metal."

He answered back, "Don't fuck with it. Come over here and take care of these gooks."

Baker moved quickly toward the cows. He hesitated as the cow moved. There was tension in Baker's face.

"Look what I found, private, home-made hand grenades. A shit load of them. I say about a hundred of those babies."

The hand grenades were made by stuffing black powder into Coca-Cola cans. When exploded, they would send hundreds of barbed wire points into the body.

My mind was on the hand grenades and not the prisoners when one of the Vietnamese ran towards the bush. "Dung lai, dung lai," I shouted to stop.

"Waste him," Sergeant Baker shouted at me.

Bang. I missed the Vietnamese by a hair. I quickly took aim at the center of his small back.

Bang. Bang. Bang. Bullets ripped his back. He fell down on his face. The two bullets that hit ripped his whole right side open. His body was still moving when I got there.

Down the trail the squad was double timing toward me and the dead Vietnamese. Private Davis was the first to reach me. He jumped with joy as he kicked the dead Vietnamese. He threw down an ace of spades which read, "Greetings from the 101st Airborne Division."

"All right, Sullivan, you got your first gook. Your first ear."

The ham and eggs suddenly rushed out between my teeth. I laid down my sixteen and got on my knees to vomit.

Davis came up and tapped me on the shoulder and said, "He's just a fucking gook. One less to worry about."

"Get away from me, you fucking ass. That's a boy, not some animal." I was sweating and shaking. I felt sick.. I was frightened. I just killed a sixteen-year- old boy. I got back on my knees and started crying.

Sergeant Baker shouted at Davis, "move your ass and get over there with the prisoner." Sergeant Baker came up to me and said, "Are you okay? Sullivan, the first one is the worst You'll do a lot more killing before you'll leave this part of the world."

I knew Baker was feeling bad for me because he went through this too. The prisoner stared at me with a blank. He got on his knees as Davis pointed his sixteen at his head.

The prisoner would be important to headquarters. The interpreter would interrogate the young boy. The chattering began as Lieutenant Nguyen took his machete in his right hand. He grasped the boy's hand and kneeled next to him. He stretched his hand out and…chop. Three fingers came off. Chop. Two more came off. The young boy screamed.

We found information in a brown canvas knapsack buried in the ground. The pack produced a wad of documents.

Later I learned that the boys were brothers. He showed no pain from the loss of his brother. I stroked the young boy's head as I placed a fresh bandage on his hand. He showed no compassion. His black eyes just stared at the darkness. I felt like shit. Two dead Americans full of maggots, one dead Vietnamese, and one young boy with his fingers missing.

We were in no-man's land, just a few miles from the Laotian border. Lieutenant Nguyen didn't bother to administer aid to the young boy. The boy rose slowly and stared as Nguyen as he placed his forty-five in his mouth and Boom. I screamed as his body fell back with his face missing.

From the distance roared the chopper blades.

"Sarge, they want you on the horn."

The choppers were on their way to pick us up. "Blue Dragon, this is Blue Dog, can you read me?

"Blue Dragon, this is Blue Dog...."

I felt sick and disoriented, like I was living in a dream and standing in an unreal world. It was more horrible than I had imagined, and I knew it was just the beginning.

CHAPTER 5

Dear Dad,

Yesterday I contributed directly to the war effort. I killed a sixteen-year old Vietnamese boy. I feel so bad about what I did, I had nightmares last night. I'll go see the company chaplain today. Dad, please don't tell mom about all this. I don't want to worry her. Tell her that I'm in a safe place.

Vietnam is a beautiful country. There're mountains like California. The beaches are beautiful also. Well Dad, a year is a long tour to be somewhere where there's fighting. If by chance something happens to me while I'm over here, I don't want you or Mom to feel bitter. Remember, I'm here to fight communism. I will die for my freedom and beliefs.

Your son,
Charlie

Rain clouds swept down the mountainside, hanging over the morning like dull lead. It was still humid and hot down below. The monsoon was on its way, and the scuttlebutt was that we were going on a full alert and ready for a large-scale operation. Some distance away, artillery fire rumbled. B-29 bombers roared overhead from their base in Guam. Their targets were somewhere in the Northern Sector of Vietnam. Some distance to the south, were the sky was clear, a few gunships skimmed over the ridge-line. Moments later, rockets rumbled on the mountain ridge. More and more I realized just how real the war was.

One hundred miles south of Kontum Province, the big brass from Vietnam and America, assisted by the Korean Army, were discussing and reviewing the intelligence reports in our sector. Within a few days, one of the largest operations would be a reality, a search and destroy operation to seek and destroy the enemy.

Sergeant Baker and Captain America were on their way to the Command Post where the rest of the non-commissioned and officers waited for the scuttlebutt. There would be oil burning for the next twenty-four hours, map reading and so on. I had a bad feeling about the meeting. I was afraid I would have to kill someone again.

Most of the troopers were still asleep early in the morning when I walked down the hill. Some young war correspondent with his cameras rushed to the Command Post. He looked young and naïve – probably just how

I looked a few days earlier. The Sergeant of the Guard escorted him back to the entrance. There he sat with his cameras on the dirt. He looked like a big joke.

bbbbbbbbrrrrrrrooooooowwwwwww. Bursts from a sixty echoed in the distance. Boom. A Claymore mine was set along the perimeter western sector. bbbrrrooowww! More bursts came from the sixty. I rose slowly from the ground. The outpost was firing at water buffalo penetrating the perimeter. The war correspondent's face lit up and he ran with his cameras. Does he know how ridiculous he looks? I wondered. The men at the outpost screamed at the buffalo and threw C ration cans at the beast. They hit him and the bull kicked and jumped like his cousin at a rodeo.

The war correspondent's dialogue was rudely interrupted by the appearance of Sergeant Baker. "Hey, keep your shit together, Mr. War Correspondent and stop pestering the troops. You'll be briefed later this afternoon. Okay?"

Most of the men were freshly shaved and showered as they walked to the chow line.

I had bad news for the first platoon. "We have our first patrol."

Hours later, the platoon stood around the landing zone waiting for the choppers to pick up and drop us in no-man's land. Sergeant De La Cruz was reading the Stars and Stripes. He was calm, like nothing was going to happen. He stopped reading, gave us a queer look up and said, "Get your Goddamn flak jackets on. Zip them up and zip your fucking mouths. Listen to all instructions, and don't ask any stupid questions."

I started laughing.

"What the fuck are you laughing at Private?" Sergeant De La Cruz looked at me, irritated. "Are you still laughing?"

"No Sarge."

He gave me a dirty look and said, "Sullivan, you'll be responsible for the war correspondent. Stick to him like fly shit. If he doesn't listen, kick him in the ass."

The choppers were down on the small perimeter. Sergeant Baker and the war correspondent trotted to the landing zone. The Hueys were ready to lift off. The blades of the choppers blew grass and weeds in the air as we lifted off. The huey carried seven men, including the pilot and two gunners. The door gunners cleared their sixty machine guns. bbbrrrooowww. A burst of six rounds went into the ground. My ears popped as the sound echoed in the chopper.

Hours later, we reached our destination in a clearing somewhere near the Laotian border. A squad from the Fifth Special Forces waited in the clearing. A green flare okayed the landing. The small convoy of choppers whirled around as one by one landed. The men ran out of the choppers. Our chopper made a quick turn and down we went.

"Move your ass, Sullivan. Move. Goddamn, move. Keep your head down before some gook blows it off."

The platoon moved and set up a small perimeter to protect the choppers. The Second Lieutenant from the Special Forces me with Baker. They had a casualty with them. They were ambushed the night before a few miles back. They looked tired and hungry. The stretchers were under some bushes. One man died the night before from a chest wound. He was only in Vietnam two weeks.

A few minutes later, the choppers left with the two bodies. I saw them in the distance between the clouds. We started on our mission. I learned that we were the vanguard for the largest search and destroy operation up to date in the Vietnam War. Our mission was to locate the enemy in secrecy and establish a base and hold. Furthermore, our objective was to infiltrate the enemy and formulate plans for a successful operation. The area had been selected because of aerial reconnaissance by the French during the French and Indonesian War. It was outdated but still had valuable information.

The advance patrol objective was to dig in and wait for the division to come through the jungle. The scuttlebutt was that we were to hold at any cost, even our lives.

"You fucking Coonass." Baker was giving Davis hell. He had a pack full of C rations – no ammo, but C rations. He brought no grenades, but plenty of C's. "What the hell do you have in your bandoleer, Tootsie Rolls? You fucking dick head, what are you going to throw at the gooks? Meat and potatoes?" Sergeant Baker continued shouting at the rest of the platoon. "I pray to God that the rest of you fucking people brought ammo. This isn't a picnic. It's a fucking war. People are dying. Well, where are the rubbers and wine so we can go whoring around? You crazy bastard." It took Sergeant Baker half an hour to cool off.

The Second Lieutenant brought maps about the sector. They were several maps he wanted to study with Baker. We were about ten miles from the Laotian border and six miles from Camp Dragon, the Fifth Special Forces Outpost.

I heard the Second Lieutenant discuss the bad news. "There are about two or three company-sized hard-core North Vietnamese troops in the area. They're well equipped with AK-47s and with Chinese advisors."

"Dig them deep. I want to see assholes and elbows," Baker said. It was still early in the evening as dusk fell. It was cool and damp. Garcia and Cook took the first watch. The rain fell harder. I heard raindrops on my steel pot. Drip-drop drip-drop. I covered up with my poncho. I had a bad feeling that something was going to happen tonight.

Cook and Garcia walked about a hundred yards from the small perimeter. They placed the sixty with about four hundreds rounds between them. I hope we don't find them with their throats cut in the morning, I thought.

"Private Sullivan, stop dreaming about that cunt back home. Don't worry about it. Jody has her legs in the air about now," he said with a large grin. Deep down I knew it was true. When I received that Dear John letter in basic, it about killed me.

"Sullivan, stick with the correspondent and don't let him get in the way."

The night grew darker, a thick, palpable purple as Lightning flashed in the distance. I wondered if she did have her legs in the air. I guess she did. I wondered who was doing the driving. I covered the war correspondent with my poncho. I knew this was his first assignment.

The heat of the day came quickly. It burned through my flak jacket. I had to remove it. It had caused a rash on my shoulders, they were raw and sore. The night's rain made the morning sun like a sauna. My gopher hole was four feet deep with a good firing line in all directions. The platoon didn't bother with concealment.

I did. I was going home, back to the world, back to pizza, hamburgers, and girls.

The Viet Cong knew we were in the area. There would soon be some contact between them and us. I had my entrenching tool and bayonet on my side, just in case.

Several miles back, two companies, Alpha and Charlie, headed by Captain America and Captain Monroe, humped through the bush. This was the largest scale operation any American division had undertaken. I knew by the scuttlebutt that it would take the rest of the outfit at least three days to reach us – three long days and nights. The companies were backed by the rest of the battalion.

I feared snipers and booby-traps. The Viet Cong would be in the thick impenetrable foliage of the jungle. Our patrols made contact with the Viet Cong on a daily basis. If the North Vietnamese launched a company-sized attack all shit would fall. The Vietnamese could destroy our small band of troops. With only a few M-sixty machine guns and grenade launchers, we were up shit creek....

"Sullivan, take a walk over to Cook and Garcia and give them a hand. We'll make a stand here if we have to. And stay close to the perimeter."

"Okay Sarge."

I was walking towards the men in the outpost when Baker tapped me on the shoulder. "Be cool."

CHAPTER 6

It was a night to pray and smoke cigarettes. The night shifted eerily with moon shadows and reaching branches. I couldn't see ten feet in front of me, but in the darkness, beyond where I could see, were a thousand terrors. The night would be a long one, and I knew it could end in death.

In the early morning, the mist from the ground rose like a fog and drifted in like a cloud. I took the poncho from the correspondent who was lying on the wet ground. I covered myself and walked to the check point to keep Private Cook and Garcia company. They had the weakest location of the perimeter, out in the open with no fortification. Our whole position was vulnerable. It would have helped if we had a couple of fifties, a few makeshift booby-traps and sharpened bamboo stakes around us.

After I inspected the small perimeter, I walked through the rows of sleeping men. They were certainly snoring. I had insomnia. I began to reminisce about San Jose, California, and the girl I had left behind.

My dream faded as a burst of fire rang out. Rat-a-tat-tat. I put up my sixteen to my shoulder and locked and loaded a round. Boom. A hand flare rose in the sky and, as it illuminated, I kicked Sergeant Baker's leg. "Incoming."

There was a burst of tracers. Swoosh…and incoming mortar. One hit twenty feet from the perimeter. Swoosh… Swoosh…two more hit inside the perimeter.

Private Cook and Garcia were no more. Rat-a-tat-tat…burst from the sixty. Sergeant De La Cruz made it back by running with the sixty waist-high and firing at will. He had gone out to take a shit when the mortar came in. He was Caught with his pants down. I was almost paralyzed by fear.

Sergeant Baker grabbed my arm. "Keep your ass down. I'll be back."

I was trying to guess the size of the enemy. The first shot was fired from an automatic rifle and small forty-millimeter mortars. Swoosh…. More mortars came inside the small perimeter. Swoosh…. Swoosh….

It was raining mortars on the small perimeter. The Viet Cong returned fire with machine guns. Two or three mortars hit within inches from my hole. The ground shook, and the earth came over my head. A steady stream of tracers that looked like the Bayshore Freeway in San Francisco raced through the tree branches. It was a deadly stream of lead coming. Sergeant Baker ordered us to retreat to the secondary position. The sixties provided cover fire from the north defense. There was close fighting, and we were in danger of being overrun.

Swoosh.... More mortars came in as we moved low to the ground. The mortar barrage was heavy, and we we're the target. De La Cruz' position had a direct hit. Swoosh.... I was afraid we were being overrun. We had fire from all sides with heavy automatic rifles. We had lost one sixty. Yellow mushrooms blossomed everywhere. Smoke and fog in the air was intense. We threw smoke grenades to thicken the cover around the small perimeter. The men ran close to the ground.

The war correspondent had disappeared from the area. I knew it was my duty to watch him, but there was business at hand first – saving my own life. I threw two smoke grenades some twenty yards away for the cover. I had to find the correspondent. I crawled out of the hole on my belly like a snake, only a few inches off the ground that shook from the mortars. I left my sixteen and grabbed Baker's nine millimeter. I crawled slowly, more like a snail.

Minutes later, I reached the first position. A deadly stream of lead from both sides crossed over me. I was caught between a crossfire. One stupid mistake, that's all it would take, and I was dead. It looked like a waste of time looking for that asshole of a war correspondent. He was probably interviewing the Viet Cong. I crawled down into the hole. Minutes later, the fire ceased. The smoke and fog was heavy as I looked out into the blackness of the night. I was simultaneously relieved and anxious. I decided to stay put till it was light.

The bright sun burned my face, and sweat poured out of me. I wondered if I should move back to the secondary position or stay there and look for the correspondent.

I heard a light moan in the distance. I began to crawl farther down to where De La Cruz had his position. I still heard moaning. Rat-a-tat-tat.... It was small arms fire. The Viet Cong would try to overrun the position. I was out in the cold. Swoosh.... There were more incoming mortars. The mortar barrage started again. Swoosh.... I managed to find a hole and crawl in slow and easy.

I still heard the moan in the distance. I ignored the sound. Was it the Viet Cong or a trooper? Could it be a trap? Rat-a-tat-tat.... The machine gun fire got heavier. I hugged the ground and crawled five yards. I found De La Cruz and the war correspondent. I reached over to them. Goddam all that blood.

"Where in the fuck have you been asshole?" I didn't realize De La Cruz was missing part of his lower left leg. The correspondent was shot in the side of the face. The pair were in shock together in each others' arm. For the first time I wasn't afraid to die. I felt exhilarated. I began to suck the gun powder in the air like a drunk goes after Ripple wine. It was crazy.

Swoosh.... Rat-a-tat-tat....

From the distance I heard helicopter blades moving like thunder. Viet Cong machine gun fire began heavier toward the perimeter. The heavy lead kept the troopers down. The evacuation would be dangerous. The sound of the Chinese bugle sent a cold sweat down my back. Attack! Smoke from the grenades signaled the copter where to land. It had to be a quick one. A slight mistake in their calculation, and there would be more casualties.

Above the perimeter, helicopters circled and dove and smoke from the rockets rose from the thick bush. The copters minigun fired rapidly, tearing away leaves and tree branches. The gunship was a flying fortress. It was invulnerable to all except heavy antiaircraft fire.

The bugle still sounded, bringing chills down my spine. We three lay still as the gunship swooped down on the Viet Cong a few hundred yards away. Rat-a-tat-tat, the minigun killed three Viet Congs. Rat-a-tat-tat echoed the sixty. Sergeant Baker and some of the troopers ran toward the primary perimeter to secure it.

"Medic!" I screamed but kept my pistol ready just in case they were close to the hole. "Over here Sergeant. I need help." I had De La Cruz and the war correspondent.

The copters swooped down the treetop level, pumping heavy lead on the Viet Cong. Rockets sent heavy smoke in the air. The second strike blasted a few Viet Cong as they ran toward the perimeter. I kept my head down with one eye open and felt the wind from the copter's blades overhead. They made their pass with a rumbling of the M-sixties. The Medevacs would circle before they received the signal to land. Swoosh.... There were mortars, sometimes heavy. The copter would not make a landing until the gunship knocked out The Viet Cong mortar positions. The injured could not be Med- Evaced today. They were in bad shape. We moved back with the wounded. Evacuation was too damn dangerous. It would be a miracle if one of the copters could get through to take the wounded out. Dark clouds drifted toward us. The gunship made its last pass before leaving the small band of troopers. It would be an unhappy, cold and damp night. The monsoon rains would come heavy tonight.

The first wave of Viet Cong was repelled. Tonight they would return. There would be more dead and wounded on both sides.

Moments later, there was peace in the air as the last copter met the dark clouds in the distance.

CHAPTER 7

A light rain came down cool and fine. Raindrops thumped my helmet. The wet mist was heavy, and large clouds filled with water veiled the small distant hills. Lightning fragmented the sky, and thunder boomed in the distance. It would be a nightmare for the troopers if the rain continued. I grieved for all the dead out in the mud and rain.

Sergeant De La Cruz and the war correspondent lay still, I moved over to see how they were doing. De La Cruz' body was hard. So was the war correspondent's.

I covered them with the poncho. Yesterday they were joking and laughing, and today they were just pieces of meat. The rain came down harder. The wind picked up and made it impossible to see twenty feet away.

"Blue Dragon, this is Blue Dog. Can you read me? Blue Dragon, this is Blue Dog...."

"Gotcha loud and clear Blue Dog. Over."

"Blue Dragon this is Blue Dog. Need Medevac for bodies. Over."

"Blue Dog, this is the Dragon. Be there in fifteen minutes for the pick-up. The dead were placed in ponchos.

"Blue Dog, see your snake."

The ground flares were out in the open. The smoke grenade gave the signal to the copter to come and take the wounded – only the wounded. The dead would stay. Mortars and machine-gun fire sounded in the distance. I finally saw three Medevac choppers.

Sergeant Baker was monitoring the evacuation. He threw two more flares to guide the copters to the small landing zone. A gunship flew over. "Blue Dog, see the enemy band in the bush. Blue Dog, keep your head down and let the dragon do its stuff."

This time the Dragon had a pair of miniguns. Rat-a-tat-tat, no more Viet Cong. From the distance, the Viet Cong used automatic rifles. Rat-a-tat-tat.... The Viet Cong were camouflaged behind impenetrable foliage in the thick jungle, in small tunnels near the tree line.

The Dragon swooped down on the bush with the pair of minis. The insurgents were caught by surprise. The helicopters were unable to land because of the heavy automatic and mortar fire. The landing zone was peppered with mortar fire. Sergeant Baker moved back toward the secondary zone. "Move your ass, Sullivan. Get the men back."

I made a dash to the landing zone and made the sign of the cross. Swoosh…. Mortar fire was heavy as I ran to the landing zone. PFC Davis threw smoke grenades in the direction I was running. It gave me some cover. Rat-a-tat-tat, the Cong began to pepper the ground close to my feet. I saw small holes the lead made. Davis was behind me. I knelt on my right knee and started firing in all directions. Davis was hit in the right leg and abdomen. He fell. Rat-a-tat-tat….

Sergeant Baker made a dash in the open space toward the landing zone. He lifted Davis on his shoulders. Swoosh, at the same time one of the copters was obliterated. The chopper exploded, boom! The explosion lit the pelting rain with an orange flame. The pilot was on fire. He was strapped to the seat.

The second chopper came down. The Viet Cong were using their mortars and automatic rifles on the copter. Under fire, I moved to establish a defense with Sergeant Baker. I was weary, urging troopers to gather and protect the evacuation. Sergeant Baker administered first-aid to Davis. The second copter landed. The pilot waved us to move the wounded. Bang, bang, bang. He was hit in the face. There was blood all over the cockpit. Lead pierced the helicopter. Boom, it blew up. One copter was left – the dragon.

I saw a dozen Viet Cong out in the open. They were stabbing the dead that were left behind, shoving their bayonets in the corpses. I reached for my sixteen. Bang, bang, bang. I wasted two Viet Cong dead on their tracks.

The Viet Cong came out like ants from the bush. The Dragon swooped down on the Cong, giving them a burst of gunfire.

A Marine A-4 Skyhawk jet laid a screen of white phosphorus to cover the advancing enemy. The jet planes shrieked across the bush, delivering white bouquets of phosphorus. It shot out in the air like a large bottle rocket. The spectacular white phosphorus sent a puff of smoke. My helmet fell off my head and bounced on the ground. Automatic rifles small arm fire rattled in the distance.

The pilot from The Dragon called the air strike. The Dragon was directing the air strike as he circled the landing zone. Administering to the wounded was the main concern. The Dragon descended. The Cong began to rush the Dragon. Rat-a-tat-tat the door-gunner opened up with the minis. Five Cong lay dead in seconds. Bang, bang, two more fell on their faces. Only the seriously wounded would go. The rest would have to stay back.

The rain came down hard as I gave cover fire to The Dragon. There was pain everywhere. Bodies were still on fire from the white phosphorus. The copter lifted up and swooped away with the wounded.

There would be no grave marker for the dead —just a poncho. The dead would be stripped and left behind. The gooks or animals would take what was left. There would be no memorial.

The advancing enemy had stopped.

We gathered together to see what we were going to do. Sergeant Baker received orders to abandon the position. We were to move farther back where the advance party would meet us. I knew it would be a long hump in the bush made especially difficult carrying the wounded.

We gathered the ammo from the dead and broke the rest of the weapons we could not take. I grabbed a few AK-47s. I was careful not to move any of the dead because of the possibility of booby-traps. We made stretchers for the wounded from bamboo.

CHAPTER 8

After a few hours, we were exhausted from the march and discouraged by the torrential rain. The Viet Cong were persistent in their chase. We were cut off from the Division. The terrain was hard on the wounded. The jungle swallowed the small band of men. The thick bamboo with its four-inch quills pierced our bodies. Somewhere we knew we had to make a stand. Every hundred yards, the Viet Cong laid a mortar barrage on us. We were running with our tails between our cheeks.

There is ugliness in all wars, and Vietnam was no exception. The Viet Cong used psychological and inhuman tactics. The inhumanity I witnessed was unbelievable. The Cong cut heads off the dead we left behind and placed them along the trails and paths. The heads were stuck onto bamboo stakes. I tried to avoid the paths, so the men would not see their friends' mutilated bodies. It was grotesque.

A bugle sounded in the distance, and the gooks screamed all around. The bamboo became thicker as I ran into the Second Lieutenant from the Special Forces. His eyes dangled from his sockets and blood dripped from his neck. His swollen tongue hung from his mouth.

Twice the Viet Cong hurled a head at us as we moved through the bush – that of Sergeant De La Cruz. The men screamed from fear. It was a nightmare. The Cong were all over us. Some of the men wanted to surrender.

Sergeant Baker kicked Private Hanson in the stomach to keep him quite. "The next man who opens his mouth will get shot," he said. "Look at you. What a piss-poor bunch of men."

The Viet Cong were making a rush in the bush. I saw them run trying to draw fire. Rat-a-tat-tat, the Cong were on us. The rear were in hand-to-hand combat with the Viet Cong. I flopped down on my knees, ignoring my beheaded friend. I blasted a gook in the chest. The men from the rear were cut-off. They moved frantically through the narrow paths. They were ambushed and killed. I knew we were cut-off from the battalion. There was no recourse but to stand and fight. The order was to move one hundred yards and fight.

The battalion gave us the worst possible news. The main body was ambushed and had heavy casualties. Sergeant Baker had us move into the heavy bush and dig in. We drew bayonets. We gathered in a small circle in the heavy bamboo.

"Sergeant Baker, we need some air support. They're all around us. We're in a crossfire." I yelled at him.

Sergeant Baker was the only one to ignore the crossfire. He moved through the bamboo, giving orders to stay in pairs. A few minutes later, he was hit with an AK-47 that ripped his leg and chest into tatters. He killed two Viet Cong before falling to the ground. He crawled like some damn wounded snake on his belly. I ran out to help him. The thorny underbrush clawed my Jungle fatigues tearing my arms and legs.

"Get the fuck down, you fucking ass. Who do you think you are? John Wayne?"

"Fuck no, Sarge. Just a simple-minded asshole." He was in great pain. Most of his right leg was gone. "Let's see. Move your fucking hands." I started moving Baker toward the bush. His boot came off filled with a gallon of blood. "My God, where are you? Did you forget about us?" I prayed out loud. Our survival hung on the air strike. If it didn't come, we could be punji bait.

"Sullivan, listen to me carefully. I called the air strike on the troopers."

What?" I shouted at Baker, not believing what he had ordered.

"Listen goddamn. Move the men one hundred yards if you can. Tell them to pour their canteens over themselves and cover themselves with their ponchos. Did you hear me? That's an order, Private."

"Yes Sarge. I hear you loud and clear"

A bullet ripped open Cook's chest as we moved through the underbrush. He was the point man, cutting the grass so the men could carry the wounded. He didn't even move, just laid on his face. I reached out for Cook's arm.

"He's dead. Keep moving. Take the sixteen."

I crawled on my hands and knees and grabbed Cook's rifle and belt.

"Leave'em. He's fucking dead. You can't do anything for him."

The men bunched up against the bamboo and started digging. In a few minutes the Cong would be all over us. We heard them coming through the thick bamboo, making animal noises.

"Hold your fire until you can see those fucking gooks." I needed time to get the men in a safe place.

Sweat poured down my face. The misty rain would give us some cover, but not for long.

There was some reassurance when I heard the horn. "Blue Dog, this is Hot Mama. Can you read me? Over. Blue Dog can you read me? Over. We have a special delivery.

Bang. Bang. Some gook blew the radioman's head off.

"You sonofabitch take this and your mama and sister too."

Bang. The Gook fell over the radioman and blew up. Booby-trapped. Our chances of escape seemed nonexistent. We had no radio. We were cut off from the main body. We were doomed.

Swoosh. There was more incoming mortars. Rat-a-tat-tat.... Machine gun fire resumed. The Viet Cong vigorously penetrated the small perimeter. They made deadly assaults on the men, hurling themselves with booby traps. The Cong was moving through the bamboo and bush. Bang. Bang. I missed.

"Throw grenades. All you've got." I yelled.

Hanson blew some fucking gook's ass wide open. At the same instant, his left ear came off from a frag. Fifty yards away, a blast from a bomb of napalm sent flaming jelly gas on the gooks. The jet swooped down for a second time, burning bamboo, weeds and human flesh. I saw Jelly coming our way. I laid-down like a prairie chicken and buried my face in the mud. I felt gas burning my rear. It burned a hole in my fatigues. It was the great Vietnamese Cook-Out. Bamboo and the terrain was destroyed within seconds. I heard Vietnamese screaming. Sergeant Baker didn't move or make a sound. I didn't know if he was dead or just passed out from the pain.

"Get the fucking radio and call and tell them they're dropping jelly on us, Hinojaso yelled!"

The radioman's brains was a river of cells dripping on some beetle that survived the cook-out. Splash.... The massive hunk of brain stopped the bug in his tracks.

The radio was fifteen yards from my reach. I crawled through the burning debris as fast as I could. I was caught in the open when an A-4 Skyhawk dropped some cluster bombs, unleashing their full fury on the Viet Cong and the area. I saw assholes, elbows and just about every other organ flying through the air from the blast. Moments later, the Viet Cong retreated. The men dug themselves out from the debris.

Our objective was to find the battalion. The men were badly burned. Their faces and limbs looked like disfigured and burned clay, stuck on to their bodies at odd angles.

Chapter 9

It was a dramatic turnabout in the chase. Only a few days ago, our whole platoon was hopelessly trapped by the North Vietnamese. We managed to fight our way out and make a stand, with the help of a heavy napalm attack to stop the North Vietnamese. Exhausted, hungry and burned from the jelly, the platoon was not out of trouble. There were still pockets of Cong in spider holes.

The men were somber. They had saved some of the troopers, bringing them by two-man litters. The dead were left behind, booby-trapped. All attempts to get the troopers back were futile. For the first time, the North Vietnamese stood and fought. It wasn't the hit-and-run guerrilla tactics. It was a full-scale war.

In the pink light of dawn, the rag-tag band of men, moved through the thick bush, carrying wounded men on bamboo stretchers. The soaking monsoon rain made it difficult to carry the wounded. The booming sound in the distance was our guide to freedom. The men were dispirited, stripped naked to the waist except for helmets. Hinojosa was stripped to the waist, M-sixty machine gun in hand. Two-hundred-round belts crisscrossed around his shoulder and back. He looked like the Mexican bandit Pancho Villa.

I knew exactly what the Viet Cong were going to do. They would pick us off one by one. I looked at the bush ahead, watching and waiting for snipers.

Meanwhile, the battalion led by Captain America was overrun by the North Vietnamese Regulars. The Cong pinned down Captain Monroe's company in the thick bamboo. It was so thick, the troopers had to use machetes to cut through the bush. The North Vietnamese strength kept the two companies split from the battalion, which also was receiving Viet Cong fire from all sides. One-five-fives pounded the North Vietnamese in an effort to keep the company commanders from being overrun completely. The two companies inflicted heavy casualties on the gooks, which we were estimated as high as seven thousand troops.

Night fell quickly as the men got a rest in the thick bush. The troopers were deployed ten feet apart to get maximum firepower The M-sixty machine gun was in the middle of the men that remained. The wounded were covered with ponchos. Some of the Eagles were digging a fortification. Two hundred yards away, the gooks were preparing to launch their final blow. The Cong had AK-47s, ready to kill or be killed. They would move quickly.

The bugle sounded in the distance, deep in the bush. Sergeant Baker loaded his nine-millimeter. One fresh new magazine was fully loaded. He was in pain, but he did not lose his composure.

"Come here, Sullivan."

The rain was moderately heavy, disgusting because it seemed it would never end. I adjusted Sergeant Baker's poncho to keep him warm. Swoosh…. Suddenly the sky rained mortar fire. The bombardment started. They would pepper the position and thrust the final bayonet.

Sergeant Baker blacked-out from the pain and blood loss. The ground shook from the violent explosions. Men screamed in pain a few yards away where a mortar hit and exploded. There was a huge hole in the ground, visible when the smoke cleared. A trooper lay face-down in the mud. His arm and legs were gone.

I swung Sergeant Baker around and started crawling into a hole. Mortar fire blew dirt and debris in all directions. The mortar fire stopped.

"Here they come," yelled Hinojosa.

"Lock and load," I shouted.

Rat….a….tat….tat….tat….

The Cong were coming in force. I took aim with my sixteen and squeezed off three rounds. I pulled the trigger and blasted two gooks to Buddha's promised land. One round ripped open my flak jacket. I blasted three rounds into a gook. He fell face-down in a small mud puddle. We were surrounded and outnumbered by eight to one.

Private Hanson thrust his bayonet into a gook's chest. The bayonet went in and out cracking his chest. Bang. Bang. Hanson's head twisted form side to side.

Half of his face and neck were gone.

I discarded my empty magazine and inserted a full one with tracers. I aimed at two gooks who were rushing the perimeter. I fired and hit one in the chest, the other in the arm. A hand flare bounced off a gook as he was running. It illuminated the bush, showing bodies all over the perimeter. The gooks were retreating but would regroup.

"Fall back," I screamed at the troopers. I grabbed Sergeant Baker by the waist and lifted him over my shoulder. I tripped and stumbled over a dead gook. I scooped Baker up again. "Let's get the hell out of here." I shouted.

I was no military strategist, but I knew that we were defeated. The battalion had given us up as dead. We had no radio to report our whereabouts. The gooks had fallen back but would regroup in the early part of the morning. I stared far back into the bush for signs of the gooks. The rain finally stopped momentarily, but still was very dark.

"See anything Sullivan?" asked Hinojosa.

"Not a fucking thing."

Large mud puddles made it difficult to drag the wounded. They moaned as we moved them, and I could almost feel their pain. There was movement in the bush, some twenty-five yards away.

"Keep quite."

The tall grass split as a large object came out. It was a water buffalo. Hinojosa started laughing. The small band of men walked toward the tall grass. It was a good place to rest for the night. I stared into the darkness toward the water buffalo and the tall grass. The bull just stood there, patiently eating grass.

I was burned by the napalm and cover with sores from insect bites. All I needed was diarrhea and it would be a complete package.

And it would be a complete package, the physical discomforts, was, was the constant gnawing fear for my life and the lives of the other men.

CHAPTER 10

The troopers were sleeping when the water buffalo laid down to rest. I examined the tall grass and lit a cigarette. There was no terror in the men's faces as they lay still in the mud puddle. I found a mud hole and lay flat along the edge, feeling better except for the persistent rain.

Hours later, the water buffalo started bellowing and running through the tall grass. I knew there were gooks out there. Suddenly there was thumping on the ground behind us. Boom. Fucking grenades fell ten to fifteen yards apart. I dug my helmet deep in the mud. Sergeant Baker was in great pain and going into shock.

A volley of lead zinged above our heads. The gooks were randomly firing from the tall grass. I listened carefully, the Cong were advancing through the tall elephant grass. We gathered close together in a small circle, each with a grenade and ready to fire.

"Hand grenades," I shouted.

The troopers dropped to their knees, pulled out the pins and hurled the grenades on the gooks. The grenades exploded twenty feet apart, sending debris everywhere.

A few minutes passed. It grew quiet. The smoke was thick from the grenades. I knew we had to make our move Immediately."

We blasted with our sixteens. Rat-a-tat-tat. We gathered the wounded and started running with every last means we possessed.

"Move." I saw a clump of banana trees in front of us. "To the trees." The group gasped for air when we got to the edge of the grove. Our small band of six and two wounded were in limbo, wondering what would happen next.

Hours later, the sun peaked through the clouds sending warm rays down on the men. Our damp bodies welcomed the rays. The troopers had been running for three days without food or water, adding to our confusion. I couldn't see how we could possibly make it back to the world. We hadn't eaten, half of the men had diarrhea, and our canteens were empty.

I watched the empty field for signs of advancing Viet Cong. It had been quiet too long, and the Viet Cong were overdue.

"See anything Sullivan?" asked Hinojosa.

"Not a damn thing."

"We should send two-man teams out on a patrol down there to find out where the gooks area."

"We can't take a chance to lose any more men," I said.

"We have to get the fuck out of here." Hinojosa looked white and worried.

"I know. We're all going out at the same time."

"Look Sullivan. Those fucking gooks again. Damn, can't they leave us alone?"

I scanned the field on the other side of the grove. I saw movement from the gooks. They were close. More came out and moved through the field. A dozen more moved through the field with bamboo on their backs. The men grabbed their sixteens and took position. The last of the ammunition was in the breech ready to fire. Hinojosa's machete was next to his side.

The Viet Cong were not advancing toward us. They continued marching in the open field with a load of bamboo. I wondered what they were up to. They knew we were trapped in the grove of banana trees. Could what they were doing be more important? I wished I had a pair of binoculars.

"What are they up to, Sullivan?" Hinojosa asked.

"I don't know, but I'm itching to find out."

The troopers ate a bunch of green bananas during the day. The sun retreated, as the dark clouds covered the sky again. The wind began to gust with a light rain, giving the men a much-needed rest. Weapons were cleaned and bayonets were sharpened.

The dark day was suddenly night as the men lay still, content to wait out the war in the grove. It seemed strangely quiet without machine gun fire or the booming artillery fire in the distance. The wild water buffalo chomped the tall elephant grass. The bull would be our way out. While the beast stayed out in the open, no Viet Cong would approach. The rain stopped momentarily. I knew I had to find out what the Viet Cong were up to. It could be our way to freedom. There was no future in the grove of trees. We had to move and get away from there.

Hinojosa plastered mud on his bearded face. He looked like something out of a Halloween movie.

The old man in the moon was high between the clouds. The dark would conceal us as we moved through the trees. We had to move quickly but cautiously. There could be snipers or punji traps between the small animal paths. We took a few minutes to rest. The black clouds filled with rain darkened the eerie night.

"Look, Sullivan. All those fucking gooks."

"Where?"

"There. About a hundred yards."

The moon peeked-out from behind the rain-filled clouds and the night became a little lighter. A hundred yards away stood a half-built bamboo bridge. The swollen river's current led south. The pontoon bridge was large enough for trucks and tanks. The Viet Cong were going to counterattack the battalion in a large force. This bridge would break the battalion's back. We had to move closer, to observe the engineering of the bridge so we could destroy it.

Hours later, the moon drifted west as the night became lighter. Hinojosa and I carefully watched the gooks. There was no time to contemplate. We had to put our ideas to work.

We decided to float down the swollen river with the wounded. The current was strong, and the Viet Cong couldn't detect the men in the river. We had two hours before dawn. We had to move quickly and make a flat structure for the wounded. The structure would be fortified with webbing from our backpacks and pistol belts. We had only Hinojosa's machete and our bayonets.

Hours later, the moon sunk in the sky, and clouds darkened the night. Our small band of men were waist high in the swollen river. We had to swim with the current before the watchful eyes of the Viet Cong. There were only two who manned a captured M-sixty machine gun. The rest were sleeping. The early light and mist would shroud us enough to pass the guards on the half-built bridge. The water came up to my chest as I waded through the mud. The structure was strong enough to withstand the current. The water became high enough for me to dog-paddle, while I pushed Sergeant Baker's structure.

"Forward," I whispered. The current was stronger than we anticipated. Sergeant Baker's structure got away from me. I tried desperately to gain on the structure, but I gained not an inch. It was heading toward the right side of the bank of the river where the Viet Cong were on guard.

Let it go, Sullivan," whispered Pvt. Hinojosa.

"I can't, I going after Sergeant Baker."

The structure tangled in some brush fifty yards from the guard. Hinojosa and the rest of the men were almost even with the bridge and the Viet Cong. Hinojosa fired with his sixteen to draw fire from the gooks as they penetrated the bridge. They were home free. I managed to reach the structure where Sergeant Baker's laid. I had to move fast into the water, but the men swam to freedom. I reached the bush as I pulled Sergeant Baker to the edge. I gasped for air, picked up Baker and swung him over my shoulder. I had his nine millimeter in my right hand, finger on the trigger, ready to fire at any advancing enemy. I had to get by the M-sixty and those gooks. Tracers from the M-sixty hit the water. The men were out of trouble. The bullets were just spots in the water. The river swallowed them up as I moved through the grove of bamboo, a natural cover as I moved toward the bunker. The gooks opened fire in front of me, hitting the thick bamboo. I moved quickly as I could. More came from the tree line. I started moving closer and closer to the bunker. Closer and closer....

The gooks fired wildly into the grove of bamboo. I was detected by the guards. I removed the plastic bag from the nine millimeter. My shoulders were sore, and I felt weak. I was ten feet from the bunker. I raised my nine, and I had both of them in my sights. The pistol misfired. Click. Click. The gooks turned around and turned the M-sixty toward me. I was face to face with death. I felt like throwing up. Sweat popped out over my body, yet

I felt suddenly cold, and ached from carrying Sergeant Baker.

Bang. Bang. Bang. Bang. Bang. I fired five shots into the gooks. Two rounds went into the first gook's chest. Three rounds entered the other bastard's groin. I heard the sonofabitch moaning, grasping his crotch. I gritted my teeth and moved into the cold muddy water. I paused for a few moments, listening to that gook groan for his mamasan.

I slipped into the swollen river and started swimming, hugging Sergeant Baker across the chest. The strong current swept us south.

A great relief came over me as I scanned the river banks. It reminded me of when I used to go to Coyote when it rained, we waited for the creeks' strong current to rise. We took an inner tube to play all day at the creek. We even took fishing line with some chicken necks to catch crayfish and small perch to eat. Our camp was made from railroad tiles that we had stolen from the tracks. Our hideout was used by older guys to drink and take girls to.

What seemed like I swam hours in the strong southerly current. It would be a miracle if Sergeant Baker and I made it back to the battalion. I feared ending up in a prisoner of war camp eating nothing but rice and fish. "We're going to make it back, Sergeant Baker. Don't you worry. We're going to make it back." Even though he was passed out and couldn't hear me, it was somehow a comfort to talk to him. It made me feel less alone.

I scanned the river bank for the Viet Cong, but there was no signs of life. I felt the bottom of the river. I stopped swimming and moved toward the bank, emerged from the muddy river and crawled to the side. I was exhausted and water-logged. My left arm felt dead. I moved it back and forth to circulate the blood. I laid on the soft grass for a few minutes to recover. I had two rounds in the nine millimeter and my bayonet. I dragged Baker to the thick grove of trees. He looked dead. His wound was bad, and it was dirty.

There was no sign of war. It was peaceful. The sun was bright and warm. After all the rain, it felt like a blessing, yet I remained wary for the enemy.

There was movement in the bush as I jumped to my feet. The movement was coming nearer. Bushes broke. I got on one knee ready to fire. I crept silently toward the bush. Something was out there. I waited a few seconds and continued moving toward the bush. Damn it was Hinojosa, lying on his back smoking a cigarette.

"What took you so long, Private?" He smiled and moved over to make room for Baker.

I crouched close to him to see if he was breathing. There was no movement. "I promised I'd get you home, and I did." I checked his pulse and his wound. I knew he was dead, but I didn't want to accept it. "Can't your hear me Sarge? I got you home."

Hinojosa looked down. "He's dead, Sullivan. You know I prayed for you to the Virgin De Guadalupe. You know the Mexican Virgin Mary."

I felt my legs going out from under my body. "What are you talking about, Mexicans. What?" I said with bitterness.

My heart sank deep into the pit of my stomach. We moved deep in the bush. It was too soon for me to mourn Baker's death. Instead, his loss made me extremely frightened.

CHAPTER 11

The copters in the distance echoed in the bush as the blades whirled around the landing zone. I heard tanks and Jeeps rumbling in the bush. I was soaking wet, and my feet squished in my jungle boots. Hinojosa and I emerged where the men were lying around the clearing. The troopers were jubilant when they saw me. "All right, Sullivan made it."

Hinojosa smiled and applauded. "Well done, Sullivan. Well done."

I heard approaching copters. I saw the body bags of men and they made me sick to my stomach. There were truckloads – some young, some old. Six copters were ready to evacuate the wounded and the dead. We came closer to the copters, and a medic ran to meet us. One copter began to lift off as one came in. The medic was young and full of freckles.

"Leave him alone, asshole," I said as I laid Baker's body on the ground.

A full bird came from behind the officers who approached me. He saluted and said, "I'm putting you in for a Medal of Honor, son."

I replied, "most of the men where there too. What about those men we left out there for those damn gooks to butcher? What about them?"

"They'll receive posthumous medals, son."

"I'm not your fucking son."

He said continued talking, placing his arm around me. "Soldiers die in all wars, son.

I was surrounded by men as I got on the copter with the full bird and Baker's body. Miraculously, military strategists considered the operation successful. The catastrophe was high on both sides. The war would quickly end, so said the brass, But in the eyes of the dog soldier, there was no end in sight.

For miles, men were left wounded, dead and forgotten. The war continued in Southeast Asia. The terrain was burned with napalm and bombs. The destruction was immense to the countryside. The attitudes and opinions of the dog face were ignored.

The evacuation of the dead and wounded was by small details. There was crying and laughter. There was praying in different languages. The evacuation was a success. It was almost nightfall before the last copter left the landing zone.

I spent the next three days in Nha Trang Eight Field Hospital suffering from exhaustion and dehydration. A large man in surgical greens stood over me in a half smile.

"Hi, I'm Doctor Steinberg." The doctor reached out and touched my forehead.

"What's wrong with me Doc?"

"Just tired. Like the rest of us."

He smiled and walked off. The room was full of nurses attending to the rest of the men. Some stuck tubes and needles into their bodies. The nurses were sitting by some of the men who were missing limbs and others with bandages over their faces.

Minutes later, a young boy no more than seventeen broke into a sob and collapsed into a nurse's arms. I tried to help, but I was still to weak.

A soldier with a badly swollen face next to me said, "Don't worry, man. He lost both legs from a "Bouncing Betty."

Despite the constant pain and fear around me, I tried to remain calm. Luckily, few people experience such horror. I don't know how I would have faced it had I lost my arm or leg.

The men looked as though they were starting to accept their future. They didn't feel defeated or cheated. They were anxious to return to the world.

We talked for two hours about girlfriends and wives and about the world. We remembered drinking in the bars. They needed to talk about their handicaps and put them in perspective. I had a ceremony to attend in the next two days. They were going to place a medal on me for bravery.

Further down the hallway, the emergency room was crowded with nurses and physicians. The men called it the "meat ball room," because of the surgery performed on the wounded. It was quick, like an assembly line.

The doctor's aprons were filled with bloodstains from prior surgeries.

Father down the wooden hallway in a much larger room lay a soldier. He was stretched-out on a table, stripped and x-rayed. The room was full of doctors, nurses and technicians. Some stuck tubes and needles into his body, while others probed for fragments with their fingers. His chest and arms were an ugly mess where the blast ripped into his body. I waited and watched them work for a few moments and then returned to my bunk.

The day was beautiful, one of those days that sets the mind free from problems of the war. I saw from my window that the sky was blue and cloudless. The north foothills that surrounded Nha Trang were visible, brown with patches of gold and green vegetation. Trees waved in the light breeze.

I remember my childhood in San Jose. As a youth I always played in the orchards and vineyards beside the foothills. Many times I lay under groves of trees and daydreamed about things that only a child could. I remembered how close I was with nature, how good and free I felt just laying on the warm earth, enjoying the freedom and beauty of the east foothills. I remembered playing and running through the groves of trees with my Red Ryder BB gun, playing army.

Moments later, my daydreaming dissolved when the doctor and the army chaplain ran into the emergency room. The young soldier had died. The chaplain draped an arm around the doctor's shoulder. The chaplain walked beside the doctor to console him. Defeat was obvious on his face and in the slump of his shoulders.

"It's okay. It's okay," the chaplain slowly patted his back. "You did all that was possible to save him. The government will send the telegram to his parents, so don't worry about it."

They passed the bunks where the men were lying. The chaplain and the doctor went into the staff room.

The day was too beautiful to stay in that house of death. I needed some enjoyment. I needed a pass into town. I felt rested and good to do some drinking and some loving.

After discussing my problem with the head man at the hospital, I got a pass. He knew I was a hero and would be decorated in two days, and maybe then it would be stateside for me.

I asked some of the guys in the hospital where the best place was where I could have some fun. After a few tips where the best whores were, the guys in the hospital got together some civilian clothes – a Hawaiian shirt with green palm trees with a surfer, white sneakers and blue slacks which were too big in the waist. I looked more like a clown than the last of the big-time spenders. A Jeep waited for me in front.

The guys had great smiles on their faces. "Go do it."

The countryside was beautiful beside the beach. Before I left, the chaplain gave me two Trojan latex condoms.

The driver drove down the beach and made a u-turn in the sand toward a beach bar. I heard the GIs having great fun and loud music and laughter from the locals. Most of the soldiers were black. I got bad vibrations from most of them. I stayed just for a beer and grabbed a xich lo into downtown.

The xich lo driver gave me the grand tour of downtown Nha Trang. He was young, but he knew where all the bars were. He kept saying that each bar was "Number One."

The sidewalks were full of drunken soldiers. Nha Trang, The French Riviera of Southeast Asia, was up to its expectations. People crowded the streets. Merchants sold and bought cigarettes from the soldiers. Lambrettas were filled with young and old girls and boys. Young Vietnamese boys shined boots on the sidewalks. Students rode their bicycles to and from the university. The normal actions of everyday life made it seem impossible that such a horror was happening in the same country.

I made friends with a few guys from the First Calvary in the San Francisco Bar. It was a huge hotel that was reconstructed into a house of pleasure. The music was great, mostly from the Temptations and Smokie Robinson and The Miracles. I knew I was going to have some fun there. There were some babysans sitting with soldiers.

I wished Sergeant Baker and the rest of the platoon could be there drinking and having fun. Most of the soldiers wanted to forget the war for a few hours. Some were crying in their beers, others were sad. No one wanted to kill or see a friend killed, but until the war was over, the killing would continue. Most were physically and mentally exhausted. Some still cared. I began to alienate myself from the rest. I began to feel animosity toward the Vietnamese who were there. I started to shake. I knew there was something wrong with me even though I felt no pain. I removed myself from the table and went outside to get some fresh air.

Hours later I walked down a crowded street filled with busy markets and restaurants. I was having a bum trip. The empty look of those beheaded soldiers flashed before my eyes. I was running through the jungle with Sergeant Baker's head in my hands. I was reliving those days in the bush. Bombs went off in front of the platoon, and gooks overran the perimeter. Cobra helicopters fired their rockets. Men died. Leeches covered my face....

I stopped in front of a French restaurant where I tried to pull myself together. In front was an old mamasan with all her teeth black from beetle nuts. From the corner of her mouth, mamasan began to spit beetle juice. "Get away from me," I screamed.

"You're fucking ten," she answered.

I needed a room before the military police got me for drunk.

"Me want some girl. Can you find for me?" I asked her.

She nodded her head to follow. She smiled with those black teeth. Ten minutes later we arrived at a run-down hut made from beer cans and C ration boxes. The smell could have killed an elephant. It was like being hit by a baseball bat. The stink from the small hallway made my stomach churn. I saw snakes and spiders on the walls. The room had just a placement in the middle of the floor beside a large tubular pillow. Someone moved and demanded her money. I felt my stomach rumble like a volcano. It roared out once more, and vomit fell over the small person on the mat.

I turned and ran out into the street. I gasped for fresh air and I lit a cigarette, which burned my mouth. I staggered in the crowded street. "Gook City... Sin Loy, you sonofabitch. I made it."

Hours later I found myself in an alley with dogs and pigs. I raised my head from the shit and trash. The recurring nightmare returned. Heads and bodies came back at me screaming. I saw their bloodshot eyes popping out of their sockets. Sweat poured from my brows as I tried to collect my thoughts. I pleaded with my sanity. I huddled on the ground, my head close to my knees, begging God for help.

Someone nudged me on the shoulder. "Hey, soldier, are you okay?"

I looked at this large person, not knowing what to say. Helplessness came over me. I started to crawl like a maggot. He picked me up. I fell over into his large arms. I had no articulation in my legs. My arms crumbled onto the ground as my body followed. There was no fight in me. I laid on the dirt with the bugs, the shit, with the dead, with my friends....

CHAPTER 12

At Sunday's ceremony at Nha Trang, General William C. Westmoreland, Commander of the Forces in Vietnam, personally awarded me a Silver Star for my gallantry. He also recommended me for a Medal of Honor, the nation's highest combat award. The news media covered the ceremony from the Stars and Stripes to the New York Times.

Three days later I was flown home where I would celebrate with the folks back home. WELCOME BACK HOME CHARLIE! the posters in large letters read all along the street where I was born. Friends and family were there waiting to welcome me back. I was a war hero, a great warrior.

My father was the first to greet me at the airport. He smiled with pride and approval. He ran out with his hands out to greet me. "Son, it's good to have you back home."

"It's great to be back home, Dad."

"Damn, it's good that you're in…."

"Dad, I'm okay."

He patted me on the shoulder and then smiled again. "Mother couldn't come. She's entertaining the guests."

"It's okay Dad. I don't mind."

Fifteen minutes later, I entered the old block to see all the posters on the front yards. The front door opened, and mother came out to greet me with her outstretched arms.

Dad said, "Here's your son. Doesn't he look good?"

She had aged, with wrinkles and bags under her eyes. She embraced me warmly, a deep hug I needed. I began to cry to see friends like Uncle Charlie. The room was filled with hushes. I stared at them and felt numb, wanting to hide my emotions. I smiled and rubbed my eyes, catching Clarence in a brotherly hug.

"What's happening man?" Good you made it back.

"Me too, man." Clarence had been drinking, and he made it back toward the kitchen.

I gazed at my father. He knew I wanted to go into my room away from everyone. "Dad, I need a rest. It was a long trip from Nam."

"Sure son. Sure. Okay people, that's all for today. Charlie needs his rest. Tomorrow is another day."

I exit from the front room to my room and drew back the curtains. It grew dark as I laid on the soft bed and I forgot about the war.

Father came in with his concerned smile and said, "Forget it, son. It's over for you."

"Is it Dad? How can you forget that you killed boys?"

He rubbed his rough hands over my face and kissed me.

"Dad, I can't forget. I'm sick from the war."

"Son, you'll be all right in time," Father mumble. "You need to be with your friends. Go out and have some fun. Find a girlfriend." Father nodded. "It takes time, son. It takes time."

He walked out, closing the door.

Try to forget son. He was trying desperately to comfort me, but he was making me uncomfortable. I needed some sleep. Sleep…. Sleep…. I spent the next few days locked in my bedroom with the curtains drawn, playing old records and looking through old yearbooks. The old faces in the yearbook became the faces of the squad of men who were left in Nam. Their yearbook was The Gook Diary. Their heads were on bamboo stakes, their faces were crushed. The nightmare still hung in my mind. I slept most of the time on the floor because of the nightmares I had at night. I found myself on the floor in the morning. The sheets were soaked in sweat from the nightmares. I wondered if I would ever stop living the life of the bush and become human again.

Later that same day, I played records and smoked until there was a loud knock on the door. It was Clarence.

"Hey man what's happening?"

"Not much."

"It's Saturday. There is a concert in Livermore with the Rolling Stone and Santana. Come on, let's get loaded."

"Why don't you grow up, man, and cut that fucking hair?"

"Man, you've been gone a long time. The girls love guys with long hair."

"Man, you look like a fucking faggot."

"Come on, man, let's forget the hair. Let's go take a few joints and get high and listen to the Stones." Clarence drew back the curtains. "Man you're living in the dark ages."

"Man, you look like a bum with the long hair and that field jacket," I snapped. "Do you think I killed babies and old ladies?"

"Well, I've read in the newspapers that the bombs are killing them."

I jumped from the bed and grabbed Clarence's neck. "You sonofabitch. I had friends that those fucking gooks butchered and left for the animals and bugs. And those so-called babies I killed were trying to kill me, asshole."

"Okay. Okay. I get your drift. So cool-off. Okay man?"

The door opened and mother came in with a beer. "Charlie what's the matter with you two boys?"

"Nothing, Mom. Nothing."

"Have a beer, Clarence." Mom knew something was not right between Clarence and me. "Here, Son. There's more in the fridge."

"Hey Charlie, I'm sorry. Let's be friends like the old days. Okay?"

"Sit your ass down and drink that beer. So tell me about the concert. So the Stones will be there in Livermore?"

"Charlie, tell me about the pussy over there. How many times did you get laid? I hear that the pussy is great"

"Don't you care about anything, man, besides getting loaded?"

"That's all, man. Just getting loaded.

"You disgust me."

"Hey man, I'm just trying to get you into the world again. You're just laying in this room like a hermit."

I knew Clarence was just trying to help. "Okay man, just forget it. Okay?"

"Come on, man, let's get high and go to the concert. Okay? You'll dig it."

San Jose hadn't changed much the past six months. The grove of apricot trees were hung heavy and sweet with fruit, and the east foothills were brown and green. The snake-like road to Mt. Hamilton gave me a tremendous view of the valley. Clarence's blue and white station wagon had curtains in the back windows with paper flowers all over the outside of the car.

"Try this, man, and get a high that you won't forget." Clarence handed me a small pill.

"What the fuck is it?" I asked.

"It's LSD."

"Where did you get this shit from?"

"Haight Ashbury in Frisco."

"You mean where those fucking hippies are?"

"Yeah man. It's good stuff. It'll blow your fucking mind."

"Man, my head is fucked up from the war."

"It'll make you forget it, man. Try it. It's great."

"Forget it, man. Just keep your eyes on the road."

"Well, here's some weed. Roll'em up. Make me a super bomber."

"Make it yourself, man. Just keep your eyes on the road. On the road man."

Hours later after several joints we arrived at the outskirts of Livermore. The traffic was bumper-to-bumper. People walked along the roadside for miles. There were groups of people of ten to a hundred together. Some were drinking and some smoked marijuana. Some people were camping overnight beside the road. There were tents and sleeping bags, and people were moving through the bodies, almost like body bags in Nam.

"Why don't you park the car and let's walk to the fairgrounds?"

"Shit, man, it's about five miles." Clarence almost sounded whining.

"So get your fat ass in shape."

"Okay, whatever you want."

Clarence parked his car beside the railroad tracks. The massive wave of thousands of young people to see a concert was inconceivable. There were business transactions, people selling wine and marijuana. Five and ten dollar bags were selling at fifteen dollars. Tickets to the concert were ten dollars. He heard the instruments warming up. Clarence stopped and rolled a bomber. He wasn't the only one rolling and smoking.

"Man, it's great." Clarence said. "Let's get close to the stage. That's where the pussy is."

"Man, you're fucking crazy."

We managed to get close to the stage, close to two teen-age girls who were drinking wine. We traded some marijuana for their company and wine. The girl to my right started talking about God and peace. She was way out in space, so young and full of wine and marijuana. Her face was dingy, and she smelled like shit. Clarence mixed the wine with two LSD pills.

"Here, take some Farm. Some Boone's Farm."

I drank deeply. It tasted good and sweet. I took a second one. It went down hard and got stuck in my windpipe.

The girl grabbed it from me. "Give it here, you fuckhead."

The ten thousand people were either drunk or loaded with pills and marijuana. They passed bags and pills to each other.

"The Stones. The Stones. I'm so stoned. I have no bones." Clarence managed to remove his shirt, and he started chewing on it.

"Sit down, you asshole," I said, pulling Clarence down. "What's the matter with you fool?"

"Man, do you know how it feels being in space? It's a blast off. See, I'm a rocket. See I can fly in space."

"Sit down you fool."

The musicians moved to the platform with a bang of fireworks set off in the air. I fell to the ground. I started moving behind a couple who were up front. I started seeing red images – blood red. What did Clarence do to the wine? I wondered. My body was moving, and my mind was still.

Minutes later the music started with the Rolling Stones.

"I Can't Get No Satisfaction, I Can't Get No Satisfaction."

The people jumped and screamed as the queer-looking person with long hair and tight pants jumped on the stage.

"I Can't Get No,
I Can't Get No,
Satisfaction."

"Stand your ground, Sarge. The gooks are all around us. We need air cover. Get on the horn and get that damn air strike. I see them coming. Cook, get the sixty and cover the right perimeter."

"Charlie, what's the matter you? There aren't any Viet Cong here. You're back in the states."

"Sarge, get the radio and call for the air strike. Can't you see that the fucking gooks are around the perimeter? Where's De La Cruz and the rest of the squad, Sarge?" We need help."

"I Can't Get No,
I Can't Get No,
Satisfaction."

"Charlie, what's the matter with you?"

"Sarge, let's get back to the river and make it to the battalion. Please Sarge, get to the river. We can make it back to the world. Sarge, you can't die. We can make it. Get up. We have to make it. There. I see those fucking gooks. Garcia, watch it."

The eyes of the crowd were on Charlie. There was blood in his eyes and death all around him. Blood pulsed through his head.

"I Can't Get No,
I Can't Get No, No, No, No, No, No, No....
Satisfaction...."

Charlie ran toward the stage.... "The gooks are after me. They're all around."

"Sergeant Baker, Cook, Garcia, Davis, De La Cruz... dead. All dead."

"I can't get a hero's welcome."